3.5

EYEWITNESS CLASSICS

LITTLE
WOMEN

A DORLING KINDERSLEY BOOK

A RETELLING FOR YOUNG READERS

Project Editor Caryn Jenner
Art Editor Penny Lamprell

For Dorling Kindersley
Senior Editor Alastair Dougall
Managing Art Editor Jacquie Gulliver
Picture Research Liz Moore
Production Steve Lang

First published in Great Britain in 1999 by
Dorling Kindersley Limited, 9 Henrietta Street, London WC2E 8PS
www.dk.com

A CIP catalogue record for this book is available from the British Library.

ISBN 0-7513-6206-9
Colour reproduction by Bright Arts in Hong Kong
Printed by Graphicom in Italy

EYEWITNESS CLASSICS

LITTLE WOMEN

LOUISA MAY ALCOTT

Illustrated by
CHRIS MOLAN

Adapted by
JANE E. GERVER

DORLING KINDERSLEY

LONDON • NEW YORK • SYDNEY • DELHI

Contents

Meg

Jo

Beth

Amy

Marmee

Father

Laurie

Mr Laurence

INTRODUCTION

Louisa May Alcott was sceptical when, in 1868, her Boston publisher suggested that she write a story for girls. But she agreed to "try the experiment, for lively, simple books are much needed for girls". Louisa also needed money, for her parents and sisters relied on her financial support.

She decided that the girls she knew best were herself and her three sisters, so she based the book on her family and created Jo March as her own fictional counterpart. Like Louisa, Jo struggles between her strong-willed nature and the docile behaviour expected of girls in the 1800s. "I used to imagine my mind a room in confusion, and I was to put it in order," Louisa, aged 17, wrote in her journal. In *Little Women*, Jo feels much the same.

This Eyewitness Classic edition explores the parallels between *Little Women* and Louisa's life using quotes from her journal to reveal her deepest thoughts. The sensitive retelling is true to the style and emotion of the original, while photographs and paintings give a sense of life in New England during the American Civil War.

Now a well-loved classic, *Little Women* was an instant success. Louisa May Alcott – and her alter ego, Jo March – paved the way for strong female characters in children's literature, for *Little Women* was the first book to feature such a spirited young heroine – a girl with a mind of her own.

Jo (far right) played by Katharine Hepburn, her sisters, and Marmee, hold an important discussion in the award-winning 1933 film of *Little Women*.

Chapter one

A MERRY CHRISTMAS

"CHRISTMAS WON'T BE CHRISTMAS without presents," grumbled Jo. She and her three sisters sat knitting in the parlour, where the fire crackled cheerfully. Beth smiled. "We've got Father and Mother, and each other, anyhow."

"We won't have Father for a long time," said Jo sadly.

She didn't say "perhaps never", but each girl thought it. Though he was too old to fight in the Civil War, Mr March had enlisted as a chaplain, comforting Union soldiers.

"I wish I could help in the war," said Jo. "I am fifteen. If I were a boy I could be a soldier."

Amy wrinkled her nose. "It would be very disagreeable to sleep in a tent on the ground."

Jo laughed, imagining her prim little sister in a tent. "Mother thinks we should make sacrifices for the soldiers. But I'd dearly like a new book for Christmas. I've earnt it working for rich old Aunt March. She's so fussy! I'm sure we've all earnt something."

"I know I have, teaching those dreadful King children," Meg complained.

"It's naughty to fret, but I've got to wash dishes and keep things tidy, and that makes me cross," Beth admitted. "My hands are almost too stiff to play the piano."

Amy shook her blonde head. "I suffer most, for I've got to go to school!"

The clock struck six. Beth placed their mother's slippers by the hearth to warm.

"Those slippers are worn out," observed Jo. "Marmee must have new ones."

"I thought I'd get her a new pair with my dollar," said Beth.

"No, I shall!" cried the other girls.

"Let's give Marmee a surprise," Beth suggested. "We'll each get her something for Christmas, and not get anything for ourselves."

"How are my girls today?" called their mother's cheery voice at the door. "I was busy preparing Christmas boxes to give out tomorrow. And I've brought a treat."

"A letter! Three cheers for Father!" Jo shouted with glee.

The sisters gathered around as Mrs March read the letter aloud. At the end, Father wrote: *Give the girls my dear love. Remind them that if we all work hard, time will pass quickly. When I come back, I shall be prouder than ever of my little women.*

"Remember how you used to play *Pilgrim's Progress*?" asked Mrs March. The girls nodded. "You had many obstacles to overcome on the journey to the Celestial City. Suppose you begin again and try to overcome the obstacles inside yourselves."

"Let us do it," said Meg thoughtfully. "The story may help us."

Her sisters agreed, though Jo felt it would be easier to fight the rebels down South.

Pilgrims in an illustration from 1860

Pilgrim's Progress
In John Bunyan's novel, Pilgrim's Progress, published in 1678, the moral goodness of the characters is tested as they travel to the Celestial City, which symbolizes Heaven. Like the pilgrims in the story, the March sisters strive to be good.

The sisters gathered around as Mrs March read Father's letter aloud.

The March family walked through the snow with their parcels.

Arriving in New York harbour

American immigrants
Five million immigrants came to America between 1840 and 1870. It was not easy to adapt to a new country, and many people, like the Hummels from Germany, also had to learn a new language. Despite the hardships, America was the "land of opportunity" for the immigrants themselves and for future generations.

Rich in spirit
The March family were once quite prosperous, but lost their wealth trying to help a friend. Nevertheless, they still help those less fortunate.

Jo and her sisters found surprises under their pillows on Christmas morning. Marmee had given them each a copy of *Pilgrim's Progress*.

When they went downstairs to thank her, Marmee wasn't there.

"Your ma's visiting poor folks," Hannah, the housekeeper, said.

When Marmee finally came in from the cold, the girls thanked her for their books. "We'll read some every day," they promised.

"Merry Christmas!" said Marmee. "Before you eat, I want to tell you something. Nearby lives a poor woman and her children. They have no fire to keep them warm, and nothing to eat. My girls, will you give the Hummels your breakfast as a Christmas present?"

The girls were quite hungry by this time, having waited nearly an hour. But they offered to help, and packed up cream, muffins, buckwheat pancakes, and bread. Then the March family and Hannah walked through the snowy streets with their parcels.

At the Hummel's house, they found a sick mother, a crying baby and a group of children huddled under a ragged quilt.

"Mein Gott! It is angels come to us!" cried the mother joyfully.

"Funny angels in hoods and mittens!" said Jo.

The children laughed.

In a few minutes, it really did seem as if kind spirits had been at work. Hannah made a fire and covered the broken window panes with her shawl. Mrs March gave the mother tea and gruel, and dressed the baby in warm clothing. The girls fed the hungry children a delicious breakfast, while trying to understand their funny English.

Later, the simple meal of bread and milk the Marches ate at home tasted just as delicious. The sisters were filled with happiness at having helped those poorer than themselves.

There was more joy when Marmee opened her presents. She was surprised and touched by her daughters' gifts, for she knew there was a great deal of love tied up in the little bundles.

Still another surprise awaited. Every Christmas, the girls presented their own play, written by Jo. This year, after they had taken their bows to enthusiastic applause from their friends, they were amazed to behold the supper table laden with dishes of ice cream, cake, fruit, candies, and a huge bouquet of flowers.

"It is angels come to us!" cried the mother.

"Is it from Santa Claus?" asked Beth.

"Aunt March had a funny turn and sent it!" guessed Jo.

"Old Mr Laurence sent it," Marmee said with a smile.

"The man who lives in the big house next door?" asked Meg.

"Yes, he heard that you gave away your Christmas breakfast, and he was touched. He sent this food to make up for it," Marmee explained.

"His grandson put it into his head!" Jo exclaimed. "He seems a nice fellow, but shy. Meg is so prim she won't let me speak to him when we pass. I do mean to know him. He needs some fun, I'm sure he does."

Home entertainment
Like the March girls, Louisa May Alcott and her sisters produced their own plays. "Plays in the barn were a favourite amusement, and we dramatized the fairy tales in great style," recalled Louisa. As an adult, she wrote many plays for professional theatre.

JO'S WORLD

The story of *Little Women* takes place during the early 1860s, a time of tremendous change in the United States. The American Civil War divided the nation over the issue of slavery (see p. 42). Meanwhile, immigrants flooded into the country, increasing the population and changing the culture. Many Americans moved westwards to settle new territories, while others crowded into the cities created by the Industrial Revolution. Amid these turbulent times, girls like Jo March embraced the changes that were on the horizon for women.

Family life was considered precious – parents placed much emphasis on the needs of their children.

Changing roles in marriage
As men went out to work or off to war, women became more self-reliant in running the household. Although Marmee and her girls miss Father, they are well able to look after themselves.

A bride opens her wedding presents

The Alcotts' spice box from their home at Orchard House

Needlework
Women like Marmee made many things by hand for their homes and families. Sewing, knitting, and quilting were practical skills that mothers taught their daughters at an early age.

A 19th-century wedding quilt

Housework
Girls also learnt to cook and clean. Everything had to be done by hand. Wealthy families hired servants to do the housework. Hannah has been a housekeeper for the Marches since their more prosperous times and has become a family friend.

An iron had to be heated on a stove.

Charitable spirit

The gap between rich and poor was growing. People like the Alcotts tried to help those less well off. Louisa wrote of her parents, "Father and Mother had no money to give, but gave time, sympathy, help . . ."

A governess taught the children of a particular family, and sometimes lived with the family, too.

Women at work

Louisa's mother ran an employment service to help women find work. Wages for women were low and the kinds of work were limited, though the new factories offered fresh opportunities. Louisa held many jobs, including seamstress, maid, and teacher.

Women worked long hours in poor conditions.

Men were paid more than women for the same work.

Teaching

In *Little Women*, Meg is a governess for the children of a wealthy family. Teaching was a tradition in the Alcott family, too. Louisa, her elder sister, Anna, and their father, were all teachers at various times.

Louisa sewed by hand, although sewing machines were developed in the 1850s.

Seamstress

Throughout her life, Louisa May Alcott earnt extra money hand-sewing clothes, sheets, and pillowcases, neckties, and handkerchiefs. "Sewing won't make my fortune," she wrote in her journal, "but I can plan my stories while I work."

WOMEN'S RIGHTS

Many women were becoming more aware of the wider world outside the home through their jobs. They joined the fight against slavery, and realized that like slaves, women would have to fight for their rights. They couldn't vote, and their possessions, including children, legally belonged to their husbands. The first Women's Rights Convention took place in 1848, and by the 1860s, the movement had spread. Today, women are still campaigning for equal rights.

Call for equality

Suffrage leader Susan B Anthony was an acquaintance of Louisa May Alcott's, and encouraged her to join the campaign for women's rights.

Votes for women

Louisa May Alcott was the first woman registered to vote in Concord, Massachusetts, when women there obtained voting rights for local elections in 1879. Women across America finally won the right to vote in national elections in 1920.

*To everyone's horror,
Meg's hair came off, too!*

Kidskin gloves

Glove glamour
*Fashionable women liked to
present an elegant gloved
hand to their dance partners.
Lively country dances like
the polka and the German
step originated in Europe.*

Fashionable society
*Meg wants to look the part of
"a fine young lady" at the
Gardiners' party by wearing
the latest styles – white gloves
on her hands, high-heeled
shoes on her feet, and ringlets
in her hair.*

Chapter two

THE LAURENCE BOY

MEG AND JO WERE GOING to a New Year's Eve dance. Meg wrapped locks of her hair in paper, and Jo pinched them in smoking hot tongs.

"When I take off the papers, you'll see a cloud of ringlets," Jo promised, putting down the tongs.

But to everyone's horror, Meg's hair came off, too!

"It serves me right for trying to be fine!" cried Meg.

Her mood improved once Amy pinned the wisps for her, though her new high-heeled slippers hurt and she wished her simple poplin dress were silk instead.

Jo's maroon poplin had an old burn in the back, from standing near the fire. It had been mended, but was still visible. "You'll have to sit still so the back doesn't show," Meg told her.

"And my gloves are spoilt," Jo said. "I shall have to go without."

Meg looked mortified. "You can't dance without gloves!"

The sisters decided that they'd each wear one of Meg's nice gloves and carry one of Jo's spoilt gloves. At last they were ready.

At the Gardiners' party, Meg was soon at her ease and chatting with friends, but Jo didn't care for girlish gossip. She stood with her back to the wall and watched the goings-on. When the dancing began, she slipped into an alcove, intending to peep out in peace.

Instead, she came face to face with the Laurence boy!

"I didn't know anyone was here!" Jo stammered. "Excuse me, Mr Laurence." She prepared to back out as speedily as she had come in.

"Don't mind me," the boy said pleasantly. "And my first name is Theodore, but I like to be called Laurie. Don't you like dancing?"

Jo explained about her dress. "I'll let Meg do the pretty."

Laurie said kindly, "We can dance by ourselves in the long hall."

Jo gladly went, wishing she had two neat gloves. She and Laurie had a grand time dancing the polka and the German step.

Meg appeared in search of her sister just as Laurie was telling Jo about his boarding school in Switzerland.

"I like to be called Laurie,"
the boy said pleasantly.

Meg looked pale. "I've sprained
my ankle in my new shoes," she confessed to
Jo. "How will I ever walk home? I can hardly stand."

"I'll ask Laurie to get us a carriage," Jo said.

"Mercy, no!" exclaimed Meg. "Don't tell. Bring me a cup of coffee and I'll rest."

Jo found coffee – and promptly spilt some on her dress. Without thinking, she used Meg's glove to scrub the stain. Luckily, Laurie arrived then to help with the refreshments. Meg forgot her foot, and was forced to catch hold of Jo, with an exclamation of pain.

"You mustn't walk home," said Laurie. "Please let me take you. It is on my way."

Reluctantly, Meg agreed. Soon they were rolling along in the Laurences' luxurious carriage.

"It really seems like being a fine young lady, to come home from my party in a carriage and have a maid to wait on me!" Meg said later that night, as Jo wrapped her injured ankle.

Jo laughed. "I don't believe fine young ladies enjoy themselves a bit more than we do, in spite of our burnt hair, old gowns, one glove apiece, and slippers that sprain our ankles!"

A luxurious home
Wealthy Americans like Mr Laurence imported many furnishings from Europe, such as silk curtains, fine china, and paintings. Only very wealthy homes had a separate room for a library.

The boy next door
Laurie was born in Italy. His parents died when he was small, so his grandfather looks after him. Until recently, Laurie went to a Swiss boarding school, but now he studies with a tutor at home in preparation for college.

One snowy afternoon, Jo saw Laurie at the window.

Jo did not see Laurie for several days after the dance. Then one snowy afternoon, she saw him at the window of the stately stone mansion next door. She tossed a snowball at the gloomy face.

"How are you?" she called. "Are you sick?"

Laurie opened the window and croaked out hoarsely, "Better now, thank you. I've had a horrid cold, and no one visits me."

"I'll come!" declared Jo. "Shut that window like a good boy."

In a few minutes she arrived carrying Beth's kittens.

"Here I am, bag and baggage," Jo said briskly. "Mother sent her love, and Beth thought the cats would amuse you."

"Is Beth the rosy one who stays at home a good deal?" Laurie asked. "Is the pretty one Meg, and the curly-haired one Amy?"

"How do you know that?" Jo asked.

Laurie blushed. "I often hear you calling to one another," he said. "And sometimes you forget to close your parlour curtain and when the lamps are lighted I can see inside. Your mother looks so sweet, I can't help watching. I haven't got a mother, you know."

Laurie's words touched Jo. "We'll never draw the curtain again," she said gently. "But instead of peeping, why don't you come over? Mother would do you heaps of good. Beth would play the piano and Amy would dance. And you'd laugh at the plays Meg and I put on."

She went on to tell funny stories about helping old Aunt March until Laurie was red with laughter. Then they got to talking about books. To Jo's delight, she found that Laurie loved them too, and had read even more than herself.

"Come and see our library," Laurie suggested. "Grandpa is out, so you needn't be afraid."

"I'm not afraid of anything!" Jo declared.

The library was lined with books, to Jo's amazement. When the doctor arrived to examine Laurie, Jo happily amused herself. She was standing in front of a portrait of Laurie's grandfather when the library door opened.

Without turning, she said firmly, "I wouldn't be afraid of your grandfather. He's got kind eyes."

"Thank you, ma'am," said a gruff voice behind her, and there stood old Mr Laurence!

"Thank you, ma'am," said a gruff voice behind Jo.

"So you're not afraid of me?" he asked.
Jo blushed, but Mr Laurence laughed and shook her hand.
Soon she was chatting happily with the old gentleman.

He invited Jo to tea, and during the meal, the change in
his grandson did not escape him. There was life in the
boy's face now and merriment in his laugh.

"Goodnight, Dr Jo," Mr Laurence said, as Jo departed.
"You will come again, I hope?" asked Laurie.
"If you promise to come and see us after you are well,"
Jo replied with a smile. "Goodnight, Laurie."

Winter wonderland
A close friendship quickly develops between Laurie and the March girls as they enjoy sleigh-rides and ice-skating in the snowy Massachusetts countryside.

A new friendship grew between the Laurences and the Marches, with sleigh-rides, skating, and parties! Meg enjoyed the Laurences' conservatory; Jo browsed in their library; and Amy admired their magnificent paintings.

Timid Beth yearned to play the grand piano, but she was too fearful to go next door. Mr Laurence set about mending matters.

"The boy neglects his music, and the piano suffers for want of use," Mr Laurence told Mrs March, loudly enough so Beth could hear. "Wouldn't your girls like to practise on it? They can run in at any time, but if they don't care to come, then never mind." He rose as if to go, and a little hand slipped into his.

"Oh, sir! They do care, very much!" Beth said earnestly.

The old gentleman stroked her hair, saying softly, "I once had a little granddaughter with eyes like these. God bless you!"

Then he went home again in a great hurry.

Next day, Beth quietly made her way to the Laurences' drawing room. Once she began to play, she forgot her fear. The piano music was like the voice of a beloved friend.

After that, Beth slipped through the hedge between the two houses nearly every day. She never knew that Mr Laurence opened his study doors to listen, or that new music was put there especially for her.

"Mother, I'm going to make Mr. Laurence a pair of slippers," Beth announced one day. "He is so kind that I must thank him."

Beth worked hard on the slippers. Then with Laurie's help she smuggled them onto the study table.

The next afternoon, a surprise awaited Beth when she returned home from her errands. In the parlour stood a little piano, with a letter to "Miss Elizabeth March" lying on the glossy lid!

Jo read the thank-you note to Beth, who was quite overcome.

I have never had a pair of slippers that suited me so well as yours. Allow "the old gentleman" to thank you by sending you something which once belonged to the little granddaughter he lost.

"Laurie told me how fond his grandfather was of the child who died," said Jo. "And Beth, he's given you her piano!"

Beth lovingly touched the keys and pressed the shiny pedals.

"You'll have to go and thank him," said Jo, half-joking.

"I'll go now before I get frightened," Beth said bravely. She walked to the Laurences' house and knocked on the study door.

A gruff voice called out, "Come in!" and Beth entered.

"I came to thank you," she began.

Then, remembering that he had lost the little girl he loved, she put both arms around Mr Laurence's neck and kissed him. Mr Laurence felt as if he had gotten his own granddaughter back again and Beth ceased to fear him from that moment.

Victorian piano
Louisa May Alcott's younger sister, Lizzie, loved playing the piano. Like Beth March, Lizzie played while the rest of the family sang.

Beth lovingly touched the keys and pressed the shiny pedals.

This unrefined sugar is called "demarara"

Pickled limes
Made by preserving limes in a jar with sugar and water for several weeks, pickled limes are a sticky treat.

Chapter three

BURDENS

"I'M DREADFULLY IN DEBT," Amy said one day. "I owe at least a dozen pickled limes to girls at school and I haven't any money." Meg grinned. "Are limes the fashion now?" she asked.

"The girls give pickled limes to all their friends," Amy explained. "They treat by turns. I've had ever so many, but haven't been able to return them."

Meg handed Amy a coin from her purse. "Here's some money to pay off your debts."

The next day at school, the rumour circulated that Amy March had twenty-four delicious limes in her desk and was going to treat! Katy invited her to a party.

Mr Davis said, "Miss March, hold out your hand."

Mary insisted on lending Amy her watch until recess. And Jenny Snow offered to give her the answers to certain sums. But Amy had not forgotten how Jenny had previously teased her about her lack of limes. Now Amy crushed the girl's hopes. She sniffed, "You needn't be so polite all of a sudden, Jenny, for you won't get any."

That day, Amy's map drawings were praised in class, and she was filled with pride. But Jenny, already insulted, was now jealous as well. She privately informed the teacher, Mr Davis, that Amy March had pickled limes in her desk.

Mr Davis had already banned chewing gum and pickled limes from the classroom. And he had vowed to cane the first person who was found breaking the rule.

He rapped on his desk. "Miss March, come here. Bring the limes from your desk and throw them out of the window."

Free education
"Common schools" gave free education to primary school children. Teachers often used a rod or a cane to discipline pupils. As a teacher herself, Louisa May Alcott did not believe in physical punishment.

Ashamed and angry, Amy obeyed her teacher. When she was done, Mr Davis said, "I never break my word, young ladies. Miss March, hold out your hand."

Several stinging blows fell on Amy's little palm. She bore them without flinching, though it was the first time in her life she had ever been struck. Her humiliation continued. Mr Davis made her stand on a platform to face the entire class.

A bitter sense of wrong, and the thought of Jenny, helped Amy to bear the humiliation for fifteen long minutes.

When she was dismissed at last, Amy went directly home. Upon hearing the sad story, Mrs March looked disturbed.

"I don't approve of Mr Davis's teaching methods," she declared. "Amy, you may study a little every day at home with Beth from now on. But I am not sorry you lost the limes. You broke the rules and deserved some punishment."

"Are you glad I was disgraced?" cried Amy.

"It may do you good," replied her mother. "You are becoming conceited, my dear, and must correct it. There is no need to parade your virtues. For the great charm of all power is modesty. Real talent or goodness will not be overlooked for long."

The fairy queen's yellow hair reminded Jo of Amy.

Edwin Forrest, 19th-Century actor

Stars of the theatre
As teenagers, Louisa May Alcott and her sister, Anna, wanted to be famous actors like Edwin Forrest or Fanny Kemble. "Mother says we are too young," Louisa wrote.

One Saturday, Amy found Jo and Meg preparing to go out. She saw Meg slip a fan into her pocket. "You girls are going to the theatre with Laurie, aren't you? I shall go, too!"

"No you won't! You'll just stay here," Jo scolded crossly.

She pulled Meg downstairs, leaving behind their wailing sister.

"You'll be sorry for this, Jo March!" threatened Amy.

"Fiddlesticks!" shouted Jo, slamming the door.

The Seven Castles of the Diamond Lake was wonderful, but the fairy queen's yellow hair reminded Jo of Amy. Jo could not enjoy herself.

Late the next afternoon, Jo burst into the parlour. "Has anyone taken my fairy stories that I've been writing?" she demanded.

"No," said Meg and Beth, looking surprised. Amy said nothing.

"You know something about it, and you'd better tell at once," Jo said, giving her little sister a shake. "Give it back, Amy."

"You'll never get your silly old story back!" cried Amy. "I burnt it!"

Jo turned pale. "You've burnt it?" she said in disbelief.

"I said you'd be sorry for being cross yesterday," Amy declared.

Jo shook her violently, crying, "You wicked girl! I worked on that story book for years and I was going to finish it before Father got home. Now it's gone and I can never write it again. I'll never forgive you, Amy!" With that, she ran upstairs.

When Mrs March came home and heard the story, she soon made Amy realize the wrong she had done her sister. Jo appeared for supper, looking grim. It took all of Amy's courage to apologize.

"Please forgive me, Jo. I'm very, very sorry," she said.

"I shall never forgive you," Jo declared.

As Jo received her good-night kiss, Mrs March whispered, "Don't let the sun go down upon your anger. Forgive, and help each other."

Jo wanted to cry all her grief and anger away, but Amy was listening. So she said gruffly, "It was an abominable thing, and she doesn't deserve to be forgiven!" and marched off to bed.

A night at the theatre in New York City

Melodramas
Louisa May Alcott's favourite plays were highly emotional melodramas, which made the audience both laugh and cry. The Seven Castles of the Diamond Lake may be based on a real melodrama.

The next day, Jo went out to ice-skate with Laurie when she got home from Aunt March's.

"I want to go skating, too," Amy said. "But it's no use asking a cross patch to take me."

"You were very naughty," Meg pointed out. "But she might forgive you now."

Amy ran after Jo and Laurie, who reached the river before her. Laurie did not even see her, for he had skated ahead to see if the ice was sound.

Jo heard Amy panting from her run, but she didn't turn to look. Instead, she zigzagged down the river, taking a bitter, unhappy sort of satisfaction in her sister's troubles.

"Keep near the shore!" Laurie shouted, as he turned the bend. "It isn't safe in the middle."

Jo heard him, but Amy did not catch a word.

"Let her take care of herself," a little demon whispered in Jo's ear. Laurie had vanished round the bend. Jo was just at the turn, and Amy was striking out towards the smoother ice in the middle of the river.

Something made Jo turn around, just in time to see Amy throw up her hands and crash through the rotten ice! The splash of water and Amy's cry made Jo's heart stand still. She tried to call for Laurie, but she had no voice. For a second she stared, terrified, at Amy's blue hood above the black water.

Then Laurie rushed by, shouting for her to bring a rail. Jo blindly obeyed, dragging a rail from the fence. Laurie lay on the ice, holding Amy up with his arm. Together they pulled her out, and brought her home shivering and crying.

Laurie held Amy up with his arm. Together, he and Jo pulled her out.

"Are you sure she is safe?" Jo tearfully asked Marmee that evening. She looked down at Amy, wrapped in blankets and sleeping peacefully. "It's my dreadful temper! I try to cure it, but it breaks out worse than ever! Oh Mother, what shall I do?"

"Never get tired of trying, and never think it is impossible to conquer your faults," Mrs March said tenderly. "Remember this day, Jo. And resolve that you will never know another like it. Your father helped me over the years to control my own temper. I miss him very much."

"Your temper, Mother?" said Jo in surprise. "Why, you are never angry."

"I have learnt not to show it," Marmee told her. "And I still hope to learn not to feel it."

Jo felt comforted by the sympathy and confidence given to her, and strengthened her resolution to mend her temper. Just then, Amy sighed in her sleep. Jo spoke softly.

"I let the sun go down on my anger. If it hadn't been for Laurie, it might have been too late!"

As if she heard, Amy opened her eyes and held out her arms with a smile. Jo hugged her close, and everything was forgiven and forgotten in one hearty kiss!

Chapter four

Experiments

A silk fan with an ivory frame

Fancy fans
Made of silk or ornamental feathers, a fan was a useful accessory. Gossiping women could observe their quarry over the tops of their fans, while Meg could use hers to hide her blushing face.

Silk gown

Fine frocks
The finest gowns were made of silk. But Meg's best dress is made of a cheaper fabric called "tarleton", a kind of cotton. Wearing a corset and petticoat under a dress created a "perfect" figure.

Love versus money
A grand ball was the perfect occasion for matchmaking. Money and social status had long been top priorities for a couple, but by the mid-1800s, love was becoming a more important consideration.

IN APRIL, MEG VISITED the Moffats. Annie Moffat, Meg, and Sallie Gardiner shopped and rode each day. In the evenings, they went to the theatre and opera. Meg tried not to be envious, but she remembered when her own family was prosperous, before Mr March had lost his fortune trying to help a friend.

The Moffats planned two parties during Meg's stay. For the small party, Meg wore her white cotton tarleton. The other girls glanced at it, then at each other. Meg's cheeks burnt. She did not like pity.

A box of flowers arrived just then, with a note for Meg.

"Who are they from?" cried the girls, fluttering about.

"The note is from Mother, and the flowers from Laurie," said Meg. She was pleased they had not forgotten her.

"Oh, indeed!" Annie remarked, with a funny look.

Meg enjoyed the party, and received compliments for her singing and dancing. But her mood changed upon overhearing some gossip.

"The Laurence boy would be grand for one of those girls."

"Mrs M has laid her plans," said Mrs Moffat's voice.

"I'll lend her a stylish dress for the big party. I don't believe she'd mind. After all, that dowdy tarleton is all she's got."

"And I'll ask young Laurence to come," said Annie's sister, Belle.

Meg bristled at this foolish gossip. She'd heard enough. She certainly wasn't friends with Laurie because of his money!

The next day, however, Meg noticed that her friends treated her with more respect. And when Belle offered to turn her into "a little beauty" for the ball on the following evening, Meg couldn't resist.

Belle curled Meg's hair, polished her arms with powder, and coloured her lips with pink cream. She dressed Meg in a blue silk gown, and adorned it with silver filigree jewellery and a plumy fan.

The clothes acted like a charm. Everyone seemed to take an interest in Meg that night. In the midst of flirting, she spied Laurie across the room. He looked at her with surprise.

"You look so unlike yourself, Meg," he said.

"The girls dressed me up for fun," she told him. "Don't you like it?"

"I don't like fuss and feathers," said Laurie.

Meg walked away, her feelings ruffled. Then she overheard someone say, "They're making a fool of that girl. She's nothing but a doll tonight."

Meg wished she'd worn her own dress. Though she made up with Laurie and joined in the dancing, the fun had gone out of the party.

Glad to be home a few days later, Meg told Marmee and Jo about her trip. "I was flattered and let them make a fool of me," she confessed. "I am so ashamed." Then she told them of the gossip.

"Learn to value the praise which is worth having," Mrs March advised. "In fact, I do have plans for my girls. I want you to be loved and respected, and to lead useful lives. Money is not the only prize to strive for."

Meg overheard someone say, "They're making a fool of that girl."

27

Mr Pickwick addresses the members of the Pickwick Club.

The Pickwick Club

The Pickwick Papers, *published in 1837, was the first novel by Charles Dickens. The "Papers" of the title tell of the adventures of the members of a London club. Like the March girls, Louisa May Alcott and her sisters wrote their own Pickwick Portfolio.*

Costume trunk

Louisa May Alcott and her sisters used this costume trunk for the plays that they produced at Orchard House. They probably also used it to hold the costumes for their own Pickwick Club.

The Marches spent fine spring afternoons gardening and rowing on the river. Rainy days were spent indoors. As secret societies were the fashion, the girls created their own Pickwick Club, inspired by a popular book called *The Pickwick Papers,* by Charles Dickens.

The club met on Saturday evenings in the garret at the top of the house. Meg, as the eldest, played the president, Samuel Pickwick. Jo was Augustus Snodgrass, who edited their weekly newspaper. Rosy Beth reminded her sisters of Tracy Tupman. Amy, who always tried to do what she couldn't, was Nathaniel Winkle.

The president began each meeting by reading aloud *The Pickwick Portfolio.* The newspaper was filled with original tales, poetry, funny advertisements and hints, all written by the members.

"Meg-Good. Jo-Bad. Beth-Very Good. Amy-Middling," Pickwick finished as usual one evening by reading the report of the members.

Snodgrass rose. "Mr President and gentlemen, I propose the admission of a new member, Mr Theodore Laurence. Laurie would add to the spirit of the club and the literary value of the paper."

"We don't want any boys here," Mr Winkle declared. "This is a club for ladies only, and we wish it to remain private and proper."

"I'm afraid he'll laugh and make fun," Pickwick admitted.

Snodgrass bounced up. "Sir, I give you my word, Laurie won't do anything of the sort! He does so much for us, the least that we can do is offer him a place here."

"We ought to do it, even if we are afraid. I say he may come, and his grandpa too, if he likes," Tupman said boldly.

Jo took a vote. "Aye!" said three voices at once.

"Good! Now allow me to present the new member!"

Jo flung open the closet to reveal Laurie seated on a rag bag. He was flushed and twinkling, and trying not to laugh.

"You rascals!" cried Pickwick, Tupman and Winkle.

"Allow me to introduce myself as Sam Weller, your very humble servant," said Laurie, as he saluted the other members. "Please forgive my faithful friend, Mr Snodgrass. He is not to be blamed for this trick. I planned it myself." He nodded to the President, Mr Pickwick. "On my honour, sir, I will never play such a trick again."

"Hear, hear! Go on!" called the members.

"In order to promote friendship between neighbours, I have set up a post office in the hedge," Laurie continued. "It's an old birdhouse, and it will hold all sorts of things. Here is your key." He placed it on the table, and sat down to great applause.

That night, the meeting of the Pickwick Club was especially lively, and it ended with three cheers for the new member. Sam Weller was a devoted, well-behaved, and jovial member of the Pickwick Club.

The post office was a wonderful thing. Poetry and pickles, gingerbread, music, and even puppies all passed through it. Old Mr Laurence enjoyed sending funny telegrams, and his gardener even sent Hannah a love note.

They all laughed when the secret was revealed, never dreaming how many love letters their little post office would hold in the future!

*Jo revealed Laurie
seated on a rag bag
in the closet.*

Jo returned home from the market, pleased with her bargains.

Cast-iron cookstove   Logs for burning

The Alcotts' kitchen
The Alcotts' kitchen at Orchard House still contains many original housewares. The stove was used both for cooking and for heating. In summer, the kitchen could be stiflingly hot!

"The Kings are off to the seashore," said Meg on the first of June.

"Aunt March went away today, too!" said Jo. "I'm free!"

"Let's not do lessons, but play instead," Amy said to Beth.

"May we, Mother? May we spend our vacations doing nothing?" they asked, turning to Mrs March who was busy sewing.

"You may all try your experiment for a week and see how you like it," Mrs March said. "I think you girls will find that all play and no work is as bad as all work and no play."

Next morning, Meg slept late. Jo spent the morning boating and the afternoon reading in the apple tree. Beth rummaged through her closet, but left things topsy-turvy. Amy took a walk, got caught in a shower, and came home dripping.

By tea-time Meg was cross, having bought muslin that didn't wash well. Jo had a sunburnt nose and a headache. Beth was worried by her messy closet and from trying to learn several songs at once. Amy didn't know what to wear to a party, since her best frock was ruined. But the girls assured their mother that the experiment was working well. Marmee smiled, said nothing, and kept the household running with Hannah's help.

As the days wore on, the girls grew bored. By Friday, they were all glad that the week was nearly done.

Saturday morning, Mrs March informed Meg that Hannah had the day off. "And I'm going out to dinner myself, so you girls will have to take care of things here," she told them.

"That's easy enough to do. I'm aching for some new amusement!" Jo said eagerly when she heard this.

Meg's breakfast was not a success: bitter tea and scorched omelettes.

"I shall make dinner and invite Laurie," Jo offered, though she knew even less about cooking than Meg.

Meanwhile Beth sat sobbing in the parlour. She had forgotten to feed her canary, Pip, who now lay dead in his cage.

"Warm him in the oven; maybe he will revive," Amy said.

"He's been starved – he shan't be baked! I'll have to bury him," Beth said sadly. "Oh, Pip! How could I be so cruel?"

"Don't cry," Jo soothed. "We'll have a nice funeral after dinner."

In the kitchen, Jo discovered that the fire had gone out in the stove. Having rekindled it, she decided to go to the market while the stove heated up again. Jo returned home from the market, pleased with her bargains. She set to work. The asparagus boiled for an hour, and the bread burnt. The potatoes were undercooked, the dessert was lumpy, and many strawberries were unripe. Language cannot describe the anxieties and exertions that Jo underwent in the kitchen that morning.

Language cannot describe the anxieties that Jo underwent in the kitchen.

Keeping busy
Like Marmee, Louisa May Alcott's mother believed in the value of hard work. Abigail Alcott often told her girls, "Hope and keep busy."

One thing after another was tasted and left unfinished.

Meanwhile, Beth made a winding sheet for dear Pip, who lay in state in an old domino box. Then Miss Crocker came to call and said she'd stay to dinner. The girls were always kind to the gossiping woman, as she was poor and had few friends. Meg entertained her in the parlour.

Poor Jo was ready to crawl under the table during the dinner, as one thing after another was tasted and left unfinished. Amy giggled, Meg looked distressed, Miss Crocker pursed her lips, and Laurie talked and laughed with all his might to give a cheerful note to the festive scene.

butter stamp

jelly mould

egg whisk

Cooking skills
All food had to be freshly prepared by hand. Since Hannah usually cooks for the Marches, Jo and her sisters haven't had much practice.

Finally a pretty dessert was passed around: plates with rosy sugared strawberries floating in rich cream. Miss Crocker tasted it, made a wry face, and drank some water hastily. Laurie's mouth puckered slightly as he ate away manfully. Amy took a heaping spoonful, but then hid her face in her napkin and left the table.

"What is it?" asked Jo, trembling.

"Salt instead of sugar, and the cream is sour," replied Meg.

Jo groaned. She had used the wrong box on the kitchen table and had forgotten to put the milk in the ice box. She was on the verge of crying when she saw Laurie's eyes, which were merry despite his heroic efforts. The humour of it struck her and she laughed till the tears ran down her cheeks. So did the others, even Miss Crocker.

The dinner ended gaily with bread, butter, olives, and fun. Miss Crocker went on her way, eager to tell of her unusual dinner.

"I haven't the strength of mind to clear up now, so we will sober ourselves with a funeral," Jo announced. Laurie dug a grave under the ferns in the grove, and Pip was laid in and covered with moss.

Following the funeral, a grieving Beth went to lie down. The beds were not made, so she vigorously put things in order. Together, Meg and Jo cleared away the remains of their dinner. When Mrs March arrived home, she found the girls hard at work.

"Are you satisfied with your experiments, girls, or do you want another week of it?" Marmee asked that evening.

"I don't!" cried Jo. "Lounging and larking doesn't pay."

"Mother, did you go away just to see how we'd get on?" asked Meg.

"Yes, I wanted to show you what happens when everyone thinks only of herself," said Mrs March. "The comfort of all depends on each doing her share. Work is good for health and spirits, and gives a sense of power and independence better than money or fashion."

"We'll work like bees and love it, too. See if we don't!" said Jo.

Mrs March smiled. "You needn't go to the other extreme either."

She looked fondly at her daughters as each girl vowed to learn new skills. The experiment was successful!

Beth's pet
Birds, cats, and dogs were all popular pets in the 19th century. Beth is a gentle child who loves animals. She normally would have fed Pip seeds and pieces of fresh fruit and vegetables, but like her sisters, she forgets her chores during the experiment.

Winding sheet
A "winding sheet" is a piece of fabric wrapped around a dead body before it is placed in a coffin.

Pip was laid in the grave and covered with moss.

Laurie welcomed everybody, then a game of croquet got under way.

balls

mallet

hoop

Croquet

Players use a mallet to hit the balls through hoops. When a ball rolls through a hoop, the player gets an extra turn. The game began in England, and was originally called pall mall.

Yankee pride

American colonists won their independence from England in the American Revolution (1775-1783). Although Jo teases Fred, the two countries became close allies.

Chapter five

CAMP LAURENCE

"MAIL FOR MISS MEG MARCH," Beth said one July day, distributing items from the little post office. "That's strange. I left a pair of gloves next door, but here is only one returned," Meg said. "I hate odd gloves."

"Laurie's sent us an invitation for a picnic!" Jo cried delightedly.

Next morning, the March girls met Laurie's guests, who were visiting from England. Kate Vaughn was twenty; the twins, Frank and Fred were Jo's age; and Grace was the youngest. They rowed down the river to the meadow in two boats. Meg sat with Laurie's tutor, John Brooke, a serious young man with handsome brown eyes and quiet manners. When they arrived, Laurie welcomed everybody to "Camp Laurence", then a game of croquet got under way.

The English played well, but the Americans played better. Near the end of the game, Fred's ball stopped on the wrong side of a hoop. He gave the ball a nudge with his shoe, and it rolled through.

"You pushed it! I saw you; it's my turn now," cried Jo.

"I didn't move it. The ball rolled through," Fred protested, and with his extra turn, he hit Jo's ball away from the hoop.

"Americans don't cheat, but I see that you do," Jo muttered angrily.

She retrieved her ball, then patiently managed to win the game for her team with a clever stroke.

"Yankees are generous to their enemies, especially when they beat them," she said to Fred.

"Good for you, Jo!" Laurie whispered to her. "He did cheat, I saw him. But he won't do it again."

"I'm glad you kept your temper, Jo," Meg told her approvingly.

After a hearty lunch, they all settled down to play Rigmarole, in which they all added to a story until it became a funny jumble of nonsense. More parlour games followed, such as Truth, in which Fred was forced to admit that he had cheated at croquet.

Meanwhile, Meg practised her German with John Brooke's help.

"I wish I liked teaching as you do," Meg told him.

Meg practised her German with John Brooke's help.

"When Laurie goes to college next year, I'll become a soldier," said John.

"Laurie and his grandfather and all of us would be sorry if you were harmed," Meg said. She looked up, and noticed that John Brooke brightened upon hearing this.

When the day ended, the little party said cordial good-byes, for the Vaughns were going to Canada. The March sisters walked home through the garden.

As Kate Vaughn watched them go, she commented, "American girls are very nice when one knows them."

"I quite agree," said Mr Brooke.

19th-century bus driver

Travelling by bus
In the 1800s, a horse-drawn omnibus was used for local public transportation. Passengers hailed the omnibus along the designated route. They could sit either inside the bus or on the roof.

Louisa May Alcott enjoyed taking walks on Boston Common.

Boston, Massachusetts
Jo probably took her stories to a newspaper in nearby Boston. Boston is the capital of the state of Massachusetts, and the biggest US city north of New York.

Ambitious girls
Like Jo, Louisa May Alcott had great dreams. "I will do something by and by … anything to help the family, and I'll be rich and famous and happy before I die …" she wrote in her journal.

Chapter six

SECRETS

DENTAL SURGEON

J O WAS VERY busy up in the garret as the October days began to grow chilly. She scribbled away, seated on the old sofa with papers spread out on a trunk. When the last page was filled, she signed her name with a flourish.

"There, I've done my best!"

She read the manuscript carefully once more, tied it up with a red ribbon, and picked up a second manuscript. Putting both in her pocket, she crept downstairs and climbed out the back window.

She swung down from the porch roof, and took a roundabout way to the road. Then Jo hailed an omnibus and rolled off to town, looking very merry and mysterious.

She walked into a building on a busy street, looked doubtfully at the dirty steps that led upstairs, and quickly left. Laurie saw her from across the street. He watched in amusement as she pulled her hat low, walked back into the building, and determinedly went upstairs.

Then Laurie saw a dentist's sign above the entrance, and decided to wait. When Jo came out, her face was very red. He ran after her.

"You got through quick!" Laurie said kindly. "Did you have a bad time, Jo? How many did you have out? Why did you go alone?"

Jo looked confused, then laughed. "I didn't want anyone to know. In fact, there are two I want to come out, but I must wait a week."

"What are you laughing at?" asked Laurie, mystified. He smiled. "I've an interesting secret and I'll tell you if you tell me yours."

"Please don't tease," said Jo. "I've left two stories with *The Spread Eagle* newspaper. The man said he'll give me his answer next week."

Laurie watched in
amusement as Jo walked
back into the building.

"Hurrah for Miss March, the authoress!" cried
Laurie. "It will be such fun to see your stories in print."

"It won't come to anything, which is why I kept quiet," Jo
added. "Now what's your secret? Play fair, or I'll never believe you!"

"I know where Meg's glove is," Laurie said. "In Brooke's pocket! Isn't that romantic?"

"No, it's horrid," Jo said. "It shouldn't be allowed. I wish you hadn't told me!"

"I thought you'd be pleased," Laurie said.

"At the idea of anybody coming to take Meg away? No, thank you."

"You'll feel better about it when somebody comes to take you away," Laurie told her.

"I'd like to see anyone try it!" cried Jo fiercely. "I don't like secrets any more."

"Come on, Jo. Race me down this hill, and you'll feel all right," Laurie suggested.

They had a splendid race. Meg passed by as they gasped for breath under the maple tree.

"You've been running, Jo," Meg scolded. "When will you stop your romping ways?"

"Not till I'm old and stiff. Don't try to make me grow up before my time," Jo begged. "It's hard
enough to have you change all of a sudden." Her lips trembled as she thought of Laurie's secret.
Jo dreaded Meg's separation from the family, which now seemed very near.

Steel-tipped pen
*Like Jo, Louisa May Alcott
would have used a steel-
tipped pen such as this one to
write her stories. She would
dip the steel tip of the pen
into an ink bottle to write.
Every time the ink ran out,
she had to dip the pen back
into the ink bottle.*

For a week or two Jo behaved so strangely that her sisters were
bewildered. She rushed to the door when the postman rang. She was
rude to Mr. Brooke whenever they met, and sat looking at Meg with
a woeful face. Laurie and she made signs to one another and talked
about "Spread Eagles" till the girls thought they had lost their wits.

A week or so after Jo climbed out of the window, Meg spotted
Laurie chasing Jo all over the garden. They disappeared into the
bower, but Meg could hear shrieks of laughter, followed by the
murmur of voices and a great flapping of newspapers. In a few
minutes, Jo came in and lay down on the sofa to read her newspaper.

"Have you anything interesting there?" asked Meg.

"Just a story," Jo replied. "It's called 'The Rival Painters'."

"Read it to us. That will keep you out of mischief," said Amy.

With a loud "ahem" and a long breath, Jo read very fast. The tale
was romantic and very sad. Most of the characters died in the end.

"Viola and Angelo are two of our favorite names; isn't that odd?"
asked Meg, wiping her eyes, for the story had a tragic finish.

"Who wrote that story?" asked Beth curiously.

Jo suddenly sat up, tossed aside the paper, and
loudly declared, "Your sister!"

*Jo read very fast.
The tale was
romantic and sad.*

"You?" cried Meg.

"It's very good," said Amy.

"I knew it! Oh Jo, I am so proud!" Beth hugged her sister.

They were all delighted, though Meg wouldn't believe it until she saw "Miss Josephine March" actually printed in the paper.

"Tell us about it! How much did you get for it? What will father say?" they clamored all in one breath, as they gathered around Jo.

"Stop jabbering and I'll tell you everything," laughed Jo. She then told her sisters how she had brought the stories to the newspaper.

"The man there said he liked them, but didn't pay beginners. He only let them print in his paper. It was good practice, he said. When the beginners improved, anyone would pay. So I let him have the two stories, and today this was sent to me! Laurie's read it and said it was good. I'll write more and get paid for the next ones. I am so happy! In time I may be able to support myself and help the girls!"

With that, Jo's breath gave out and she wept tears of joy; for to be independent and earn the praise of those she loved were her dearest wishes. This seemed to be the first step toward that happy end.

Merry's Museum

Like Jo, Louisa May Alcott had her stories published in newspapers and magazines. She was the editor of Merry's Museum, *a magazine of stories for children, when she wrote the book* Little Women *in 1868.*

Louisa's success

In 1854, Louisa May Alcott's first book, Flower Fables, *was published. She wrote in her journal, "My book came out, and people began to think that topsy-turvy Louisa would amount to something after all."*

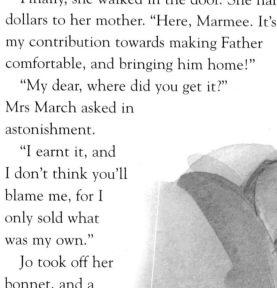

Chapter seven

THE TELEGRAM

Mrs March turned pale and sat down.

"IT'S ONE OF THOSE horrid telegraph things come for you, ma'am," Hannah said to Mrs March on a gloomy November day. Mrs March snatched the telegram, turned pale, and sat down.

Jo read the telegram aloud in a frightened voice. "Mrs March: Your husband is very ill. Come at once. Blank Hospital, Washington."

For several minutes, sobbing filled the room. Then Hannah and Mrs March pulled themselves together. Laurie rode off to Aunt March with a note asking to borrow money for the trip. The girls scattered to help their mother get ready. Jo went out to do some errands.

Some time later, Meg came upon Mr Brooke. "I'm very sorry to hear your news, Miss March," he said quietly. "I've come to offer myself as your mother's escort. Mr Laurence has work for me to do in Washington, and I will be glad to be there for her."

"How kind!" Meg said gratefully. "It will be a relief to know that someone is with her."

Everything was arranged by the time Laurie returned with money from Aunt March. But by late afternoon, Jo had still not come back. They began to get anxious.

Finally, she walked in the door. She handed twenty-five dollars to her mother. "Here, Marmee. It's my contribution towards making Father comfortable, and bringing him home!"

"My dear, where did you get it?" Mrs March asked in astonishment.

"I earnt it, and I don't think you'll blame me, for I only sold what was my own."

Jo took off her bonnet, and a cry rose up. Her beautiful long hair had been cut short!

"Your hair! How could you?" her sisters exclaimed.

"It doesn't affect the fate of the nation, so don't wail!" said Jo. "I was getting too vain about my hair in any case. I expect it will do my brains good to have that mop taken off."

Over supper, Jo told her story. "I marched into a barber's shop and asked what he would give for my hair. I said it would make a pretty wig. When I told him why I was in a hurry, his wife heard and agreed to buy it. They have a son in the army themselves."

"Didn't you feel dreadful with the first cut?" Meg asked.

"Only afterwards, when I saw all the hair laid out. The woman picked out a long lock for me. You have it, Marmee."

"Thank you," Mrs March said quietly, as she laid the chestnut lock in her desk, next to Father's short grey one.

Something in Marmee's face made the girls change the subject quickly, and they talked about the happy times they would have when Father came home to be nursed.

That night in bed, only Meg heard Jo quietly weeping, mourning the loss of her one beauty.

Electrical signals flow from telegraph wires to these electromagnets.

A message of dots and dashes is printed here.

Message-sending key

Telegraph system
In 1837, Samuel Morse developed a telegraph system with a code of dots and dashes to be transmitted along electrical wires. Long-distance communication became easier and quicker.

Jo took off her bonnet and a cry rose up.

THE AMERICAN CIVIL WAR

When Louisa May Alcott wrote *Little Women* in 1868, the country was still recovering from the American Civil War (1861-1865). Before the war, plantation owners in the Southern states had relied on slave labour to farm their crops. But many Northerners, like the Alcotts, opposed slavery. In 1860, Abraham Lincoln, a Northerner, was elected President. Angrily, the Southern states withdrew from the Union to form a separate Confederacy, and the war began.

Slaves were bought and sold at auctions

By the time of the Civil War, there were about 4 million slaves in the U.S.

Slavery
Slave traders kidnapped Africans from their homes and shipped them to America to work on plantations. The slaves had no rights and masters were often brutal.

135,000 SETS, 270,000 VOLUMES SOLD.

UNCLE TOM'S CABIN

FOR SALE HERE.

The Greatest Book of the Age.

Harriet Beecher Stowe made Northerners aware of the evils of slavery with her novel, published in 1852. Louisa May Alcott later became friends with Stowe.

Those who campaigned against slavery, like the Alcotts, were called "abolitionists". The Alcotts also sheltered runaway slaves.

Boston

New York

Washington, DC

WARRING STATES
This map shows the 'Free States' which banned slavery; the 'Slave States' which upheld slavery; and the territories which hadn't yet become states.

No slavery states

Slave states/territories 1820

Admitted as slave states 1845

Opened to slavery 1850

Opened to slavery 1854

Atlanta burns after falling to the Union army in 1864

War and technology
The new technology of the 1800s meant more efficient warfare – and far more casualties. Soldiers used quick-loading guns that were more accurate than earlier firearms. The Gatling gun, a primitive form of machine gun, was also in use.

Many soldiers were only teenagers. Brothers sometimes fought on opposite sides.

Letters home

The post was eagerly awaited by the soldiers and their families. As a war nurse, Louisa May Alcott helped wounded soldiers to write letters home.

This letter to a Confederate soldier is from his niece, Cora. "This is my first letter," she writes, "so you must excuse all mistakes … Ma says she will send me to school, when the war is over …"

A soldier's story

The war was particularly brutal, with more than 600,000 soldiers dead and many more wounded or missing. Soldiers on both sides enlisted out of a sense of duty and patriotism, but they lacked training and medical supplies. They quickly learned that there was no glory in war. Though too old to fight, Mr March joins the Union Army as a chaplain to give comfort to soldiers on the battlefield.

KEY DATES OF THE WAR

November 1860 Abraham Lincoln elected U.S. President.

1860-61 Eleven Southern states leave the Union and form the Confederate States of America.

April 1861 Confederates attack Fort Sumter; American Civil War begins.

January 1863 Union law frees slaves, but is ignored in the South.

July 1863 Union victory at Gettysburg. Both sides have huge numbers of casualties.

November 1863 Lincoln issues the Gettysburg Address, urging the preservation of the United States.

September 1864 Union army captures city of Atlanta, Georgia, and storms through South.

April 1865 Confederates surrender; Lincoln is assassinated.

Union army marches to the sea and victory

Nurse Louisa

Louisa May Alcott was one of 3,000 nurses in the Union army. She tended patients in a hospital in Washington DC until catching typhoid fever. She wrote of her experiences in *Hospital Sketches*, published in 1863.

Gone With the Wind

In the South, the mistress of the plantation had to take charge. In *Gone With the Wind*, Scarlett O'Hara must save her family home from the ravages of war.

A woman's war

About 400 women disguised themselves as men in order to fight as soldiers. Others learned to do "men's jobs" on farms and in factories. Like the March sisters, women across the country knitted blankets and sewed clothing for the soldiers. Louisa May Alcott wrote that she was "occupied violently sewing patriotic blue shirts" for the Union army. Children helped, too, knitting socks and caps to put in the packages that their mothers sent to the menfolk in the war.

Scarlett is a Southern belle who is loyal to the Confederacy

Chapter eight

DARK DAYS

THE GIRLS KEPT BUSY while Marmee was away. Though they missed her terribly, they knew that she would be the best and tenderest of nurses for Father. Mr Brooke sent daily bulletins from Washington and the girls were greatly relieved to learn that Mr March's condition was improving.

The girls replied with plump envelopes filled with news of home to cheer their parents. But after a week of virtue, the girls began to slip into old habits. Only Beth continued to do her duties faithfully. One day, she asked Meg and Jo to visit the Hummels.

"I'm too tired to go this afternoon," replied Meg, rocking comfortably as she sewed.

"And I'm not over my cold," said Jo. "Although I'm well enough to go out with Laurie," she added with an embarrassed laugh.

"Why don't you go, Beth?" asked Meg.

"I've been every day, but the baby is sick and I don't know what to do for it," Beth replied. "Besides, my own head aches and I'm tired."

"Amy will be home soon. I'm sure she will visit the Hummels for us," Meg said.

But after an hour, Amy did not come. Beth quietly put on her hood, filled her basket with food for the poor children, and went out into the chilly air.

It was late when she came back and no one saw her creep upstairs. Half an hour later, Jo found her sitting on the medicine chest in Mrs March's closet.

Beth looked very grave, with red eyes and a camphor bottle in her hand.

"What's the matter?" Jo exclaimed as Beth waved her away.

"You've had scarlet fever, haven't you?" Beth asked.

"Years ago, when Meg did. Why?"

"Oh, Jo, Mrs Hummel's baby is dead!" Beth cried with a sob. "It died in my lap!"

Jo took her sister in her arms. "I ought to have gone," she said remorsefully.

"It was so sad," Beth explained tearfully. "I saw the baby was sicker than yesterday, but Lotty said her mother had gone for the doctor. It seemed asleep, but then it gave a cry and lay very still. I tried to warm its feet, and Lotty tried to give it some milk. But the baby didn't move and then I knew it was dead. Two of the other children had sore throats, and when the doctor came, he told Mrs Hummel that they had scarlet fever. Then he told me to go home right away and take some belladonna, or I'd have the fever, too."

"No, you won't!" cried Jo, hugging her close.

"I looked in mother's book and saw it begins with headache, and sore throat. I took some belladonna and I feel better," said Beth. She laid her cold hands on her hot forehead.

"If only mother were at home!" exclaimed Jo. How far away Washington now felt!

Jo found Beth sitting on the medicine chest.

Contagious diseases
In 1856, Louisa May Alcott's younger sister, Elizabeth, caught scarlet fever while helping a poor family. Mrs Alcott then forced the family's landlord to improve their squalid living conditions.

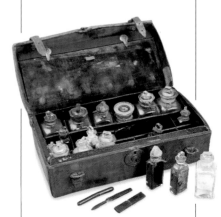

Medicine chest
Many homes had chests like this one, which held medicines such as camphor, belladonna, and arsenicum. Medicines like these came from poisonous plants, so it was vital to take small doses.

Poor Beth was much sicker than anyone but Hannah and the doctor suspected.

Scarlet fever
Scarlet fever was once a very serious disease, but today it can be treated quickly with penicillin. Patients may have a high temperature, a sore throat and a red rash.

Angel in the house
Like Jo, Louisa May Alcott cared for her own sister during her illness. She wrote a poem about Elizabeth, called "Our Angel in the House".

Hannah promptly examined Beth. "We'll have Dr Bangs take a look at you, dear," the housekeeper said kindly. "Then we'll send Amy to Aunt March's to keep her out of harm's way."

Amy rebelliously declared she would rather get sick than go to Aunt March's. Meg pleaded with her in vain. Laurie arrived to find Amy sobbing in the parlour. He listened to her tale of woe.

"Now be sensible, Amy, and hear my jolly plan," he said. "You go and stay at Aunt March's, and I'll visit you every day to tell you how Beth is. Won't that be better than moping here?"

"I don't wish to be sent off as if I'm in the way," said Amy. "I'm sure I'll be sick anyway, as I've already been with Beth all this time."

"Change of air and care will keep you well," Laurie told her. "I advise you to go soon, Amy, for scarlet fever is no joke."

"It's dull at Aunt March's, and she's so cross," complained Amy.

"It won't be dull with me popping in each day," Laurie told her. "And I promise to bring you home the minute Beth is well."

To everyone's relief, Amy reluctantly agreed to go.

"Shall I telegraph your mother about Beth?" Laurie asked Meg.

"Hannah says we mustn't, for Mother can't leave Father and it will make them anxious," Meg said. "It doesn't seem right to me, but Beth won't be sick for long and Hannah knows just what to do."

Dr Bangs arrived and confirmed that Beth had symptoms of scarlet fever, but thought she would have it lightly. However, he looked sober upon hearing the Hummel story.

Jo and Laurie escorted Amy to Aunt March's. "What do you want?" the peppery old lady asked sharply above the noise of her parrot's rude squawks.

Jo explained the reason for their visit.

"No more than I expected, if you go poking about among poor folks," Aunt March retorted. "Amy can stay and make herself useful if she isn't sick. Don't cry, child. It worries me to hear people sniff."

Poor Beth did indeed have scarlet fever, and was much sicker than anyone but Hannah and the doctor suspected. Meg stayed at home and kept house, feeling anxious and guilty when she wrote letters to her mother without mentioning the illness.

Jo devoted herself to Beth day and night. At first Beth bore her pain bravely. But after a while, she began to talk hoarsely and to play on the coverlet as if it were her piano. She tried to sing with a swollen throat, and did not recognize faces. She called pleadingly for her mother, and Jo grew frightened.

A letter from Washington only added to their troubles, for Mr March had had a relapse. He could not think of coming home for a long while. The days seemed very dark, and the house felt sad and lonely.

Pocket watch to measure pulse

Thermometer measures body heat

Stethescope magnifies body sounds

A doctor's tools
Doctors carried a bag full of medical instruments for frequent house calls. In the mid-1800s, the thermometer and stethescope were new developments, though today they are basic medical tools.

Jo devoted herself to Beth day and night.

The parrot was mischievous, pulling
Amy's hair and calling her names.

Painting by Frederick
William Lock, 1850

Aunt March
Like the Marches, the Alcotts
had some well-to-do relations.
Abigail Alcott came from a
respected Boston family called
"May". Although the Alcotts
had to borrow money from
the Mays several times, the
Mays were much more
gracious than Aunt March.

For the first time in Amy's life, she realized how much she was spoilt at home. Aunt March meant to be kind, and the well-behaved little girl pleased her. But Aunt March worried Amy with her rules and orders, her prim ways and long talks. She was quite rich, and she had never truly approved of her poorer relations. Money and manners were very important to old Aunt March.

Amy washed the cups each morning, and polished the silver till it shone. Then she dusted, and not a speck escaped Aunt March's eye! The parrot had to be fed, the lap-dog combed, and things fetched for the old lady. After chores and lessons, Amy was allowed one hour of exercise or play. She had capital times riding and walking with Laurie. After dinner, Amy read to Aunt March and did patchwork. In the evenings, Aunt March related dull stories about her youth.

Polly the parrot was mischievous, pulling Amy's hair and calling her names. Mop the dog was a fat, cross beast who snarled and yelped. And the cook was bad-tempered, too.

However, Esther, the French maid took a fancy to Amy. Esther let Amy dress up in funny, old-fashioned costumes, roam around the big house and examine the many lovely objects.

Amy became very fond of admiring Aunt March's beautiful jewels.

"Where will all these pretty things go when Aunt dies?" Amy asked Esther one day.

"To you and your sisters. It is in Madame's will," Esther answered with a smile. "I think the little turquoise ring will be given to you when you go home, for Madame approves your charming manners."

Amy resolved to earn the ring with good behaviour. Each day she prayed for Beth's recovery and tried to keep cheerful. She also asked Esther to help her write her own will. She decided that her clothes would go to Marmee, her drawings to Mr March, the turquoise ring to Meg, her toy rabbit to Jo, and her dolls to Beth. Esther and Laurie witnessed the signing of Amy's will.

Reading of a will
A will is a legal document stating what will happen to a person's possessions after his or her death. Often, the will is a secret until after the person has died. Then the will is read to the person's heirs.

"Did someone tell you about Beth wanting to give away her things?" asked Laurie.

"No. But what about Beth?" said Amy anxiously.

"She felt so ill one day that she wanted to give her things to you and Meg and Jo," Laurie said gently. "She wanted the rest of us to have locks of hair."

When he had gone, Amy prayed for Beth with streaming tears and an aching heart. She felt that a million turquoise rings would not console her if she lost her gentle little sister.

The French maid let Amy dress up in Aunt March's old-fashioned costumes.

Dr Bangs came twice a day to see Beth. Jo never stirred from her sister's side. Meg kept a telegram message in her desk, ready to send off to their mother in Washington at any minute. Everyone asked about the shy little girl, from the milkman and baker to the grocer and butcher.

On the first of December, Dr Bangs looked at Beth and held her hot hand in his own. Then he said softly to Hannah, "If Mrs March can leave her husband, she'd better be sent for."

Train travel
Steam trains were invented in England, and by 1860, the US had 30,000 miles of track laid across the huge country, revolutionizing transportation links. It would have taken Mrs March at least 15 hours to travel 450 miles from Washington to Concord. In addition, the train could have been delayed by the winter weather, making the trip even longer.

Louisa and her sister
Like Jo, Louisa May Alcott was greatly affected by her little sister's illness. "So sweet and patient and so worn, my heart is broken to see the change," she wrote in her journal. "Dear Betty is slipping away, and every hour is too precious to waste. Dear little saint! I shall be better all my life for these sad hours with you."

Jo snatched the telegram from Meg's desk, and rushed out into the wintry weather to the telegraph office to send it. She had just returned when Laurie arrived with a letter from John Brooke saying Mr March was mending again. Despite the good news, Jo looked miserable.

"I've sent for Mother," she told him. "The doctor told us to." Then Jo burst into tears, and grasped Laurie's hand as he stroked her head soothingly.

"Keep hoping for the best, Jo," he told her. "Soon your mother will be here, and then everything will be right."

"All the troubles came in a heap, and I got the heaviest part on my shoulders," Jo sighed. "Meg tries to pull fair, but she doesn't love Bethy as I do. I can't give her up! I can't!" she cried despairingly.

Laurie had to hold back the choked feeling in this throat. "I don't think Beth will die," he comforted Jo. "She's so good, and we all love her so much, I don't believe God will take her away just yet."

Laurie's words cheered Jo up, and she gratefully sipped the glass of wine that he had brought to soothe her. "You are a good doctor," she said to him. "And a good friend. How can I ever pay you?"

"I'll send in my bill, by and by," he replied. "You'll soon get something that will warm your heart better than wine."

"What is it?" asked Jo.

"I telegraphed to your mother yesterday, and Brooke answered. She'll be here tonight! Then everything will be all right. Aren't you glad I did it?" Laurie spoke very fast and excitedly. He had kept his plot a secret, for fear of disappointing the girls.

"Oh! I am so glad!" Jo cried, throwing her arms around his neck.

"Well, I got fidgety and so did Grandpa," Laurie explained. "The doctor has seemed so sober that I dashed off to the telegraph office yesterday. We thought your mother ought to know about Beth. She'll be here on the late train. I shall go and meet her."

Hannah forgave Laurie's interference when she heard the news, relieved that Mrs March would soon be home. Everyone rejoiced but Beth, who lay in a heavy stupor, only rousing now and then to mutter "Water!" with parched lips.

All day the snow fell, and Jo and Meg hovered over their sister, watching, waiting, and hoping. Night came at last, and the doctor told them that some change – for better or worse – would probably happen soon.

*"I can't give Bethy up!
I can't!" Jo cried
despairingly.*

Chapter nine

MARMEE RETURNS

LAURIE LEFT for the train station after midnight. It was past two when Jo saw that a change had come over Beth. Her face looked pale and peaceful. Hannah felt Beth's hands.

"The fever's gone and she breathes easy!" she exclaimed.

"I think she will pull through," said Dr Bangs with a smile.

As dawn broke, they heard the sound of bells at the door downstairs, then Laurie's joyful voice. "Girls! she's come!"

When Beth woke, her mother's tender face was the first thing that she saw. She smiled and nestled close into those loving arms, then she slept again. Meg and Jo fed their tired mother breakfast while she told them about John Brooke's promise to stay with their father.

Then Marmee went to Aunt March's, where she heard all about Amy's trials, and her resolution to be less selfish and more like Beth.

"Keep up your heart," she told Amy. "You will soon be home."

That evening, Jo spoke to her mother privately.

"Laurie told me that Mr Brooke likes Meg, but doesn't dare say so since she is so young and he so poor. Isn't that dreadful?"

May's bedroom at Orchard House. May was the youngest Alcott sister.

Elizabeth Alcott
Though Beth March survives in this scene, Louisa May Alcott's own sister met a different fate. "My dear Beth [Elizabeth] died this morning, after two years of patient pain," wrote Louisa in 1858.

*When Beth woke,
her mother's tender face
was the first thing that
she saw.*

"Why? Do you fancy that Meg is not interested in John?"

"Who?" cried Jo.

"Mr Brooke. I call him "John" now. He was so devoted to Father that we couldn't help getting fond of him," said Mrs March. "He was honourable about Meg, for he told us he loved her, but would earn a comfortable home before asking her to marry him. He only wanted our permission. He is an excellent young man, and we could not refuse to listen to him. But Meg is only seventeen. Your father and I agree that she shall not be married before twenty."

"I knew there was mischief brewing," Jo said with a sigh.

"Don't say anything," Mrs March warned her. "When John returns and I see them together, I can better judge Meg's feelings."

"Wouldn't you rather have her marry a rich man?" Jo asked.

"Much happiness can be had in a plain little house," said Mrs March. "I'm content to see Meg begin humbly, for she will be rich in the possession of a good man's heart. That is better than a fortune."

Meg came in just then, with a letter written to her father.

Mrs March read the letter, then gave it back to Meg. "Please add that I send John my love. He has been like a son to us."

"I am glad," Meg said, and gave her mother a goodnight kiss.

Earning a home
Before marriage, a man was expected to earn enough money to support a family. John Brooke will not be able to earn a comfortable home by working as a tutor.

Alcott breadwinners
Louisa May Alcott's family was unusual. Her father didn't earn much money publicizing his ideas on matters such as education and philosophy, so Louisa and her mother supported the family.

Meg read the letter and burst out crying.

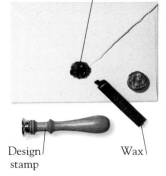

Envelope flap sealed for privacy

Design stamp   Wax

Wax seals
Laurie used a wax seal on Meg's letter. He would have lit the wick, dripping melted wax onto the envelope flap. Then he would have pressed the design stamp into the wax. Wax seals like these had been used since biblical times.

Jo tried to keep the secret as she had promised. But Laurie sensed a mystery, and guessed that it concerned Meg and Mr Brooke. Annoyed that his tutor had not confided in him, Laurie set his wits to work.

"Here's a note for you, Meg, all sealed up," said Jo a few days later. "How odd. Mine are never sealed."

Meg read the letter and burst out crying. "He didn't send it. Jo, how could you do it?" She pulled another note from her pocket. "You and Laurie wrote this letter, didn't you? How could you be so mean?"

Jo and her mother read the crumpled note. In it, John Brooke begged Meg to let him know her feelings. It ended, *I must know my fate, and implore you to send one word of hope through Laurie to your devoted John.*

"I never saw this before!" Jo protested.

"I got that first letter through Laurie, who didn't seem to know anything about it," Meg explained nervously. "I kept it secret for a few days, then I wrote back to John, saying he must speak to Father. But this letter today says he never sent any love letter at all, and that my sister Jo is playing tricks!"

Jo looked closely at both notes. "I don't believe Brooke ever saw either of these. Laurie wrote both, and keeps yours to crow over!"

While an angry Jo went to fetch Laurie from next door, Mrs March told Meg of Mr Brooke's real feelings for her.

"What are your own feelings?" she asked her daughter.

"I've been so worried," Meg confessed. "Marmee, if John doesn't know of this nonsense, let's not tell him, or anyone."

Jo returned with Laurie, and he received a stern lecture from Mrs March, then apologized most sincerely to Meg for his prank.

"I'll do anything to show how out-and-out sorry I am," said Laurie. "Brooke knew nothing of my joke, and I'll never tell him."

Meg and Mrs March forgave Laurie, but Jo hardened her heart. Only after he had gone did Jo wish she had been more forgiving.

She hurried next door to see him. He was in a very bad temper.

"Grandfather shook me for not telling what your mother wanted!" Laurie exclaimed. "But I couldn't tell without involving Meg."

A moment later, Jo confronted Mr Laurence in his library. "Laurie did do wrong, but he has confessed, and been punished quite enough. He keeps silent to protect someone else," she explained. "Write Laurie a formal apology, sir, and he will be amiable again."

Mr Laurence looked a bit ashamed, and he quickly penned a note. Jo slipped it under Laurie's door, and he was soon himself again.

But the mischief was done, and Meg remembered it after others forgot. She never talked about John Brooke, but thought of him a good deal and dreamt dreams more than ever.

"I'll do anything to show how out-and-out sorry I am," said Laurie.

Anna's courtship
Louisa May Alcott based the courtship of Meg and John Brooke on her elder sister, Anna, and John Pratt, who the sisters met at the local drama society. Anna often sat with John under their special elm tree.

Beth looked out the window at the stately snow-maiden.

*God bless you,
dear Queen Bess!
May nothing you
dismay;
But health, and
peace, and
happiness,
Be yours this
Christmas day.*

*Their dearest love
my makers laid,
Within my breast
of snow,
Accept it, and the
Alpine maid,
From Laurie
and from Jo.*

Christmas traditions
*European immigrants brought
customs like the Christmas
tree and wreath to America.
Amazingly, Santa Claus only
became part of Christmas lore
in the 20th century.*

Chapter ten

THE BEST PRESENT OF ALL

CHRISTMAS WAS COMING. Both Beth and her father were getting better, and it looked possible that Mr March would return early in the new year. Beth was now able to lie on the sofa, amusing herself with her cats and her dolls, though her limbs were so feeble that Jo had to carry her about the house.

It was a much merrier Christmas Day than a year before! Dressed in Marmee's gift, a red wool shawl, Beth looked out of the window at a comical surprise from Jo and Laurie. In the garden stood a stately snow-maiden. Crowned with holly, she held a basket of fruit and flowers in one hand and a roll of new music in the other. A new blanket was around her snowy shoulders, and a funny Christmas carol issued from her lips on a pink paper streamer.

"If only Father were here! I'm so full of happiness," Beth said contentedly as Jo carried her to the study to rest.

"So am I!" agreed Jo, glad to have a new book for Christmas.

"I'm sure I am," echoed Amy, looking at the framed engraving that her mother had given her.

"Of course I am!" cried Meg. She smoothed the silvery folds of her first silk dress, a present from Mr Laurence.

Half an hour later, Laurie opened the parlour door. "Here's another Christmas present for the March family!"

A tall man appeared, leaning on the arm of John Brooke. Though he was muffled up to his eyes, his loving family recognized him immediately! There was a stampede towards Mr March, and Meg, Jo, and Amy embraced him.

The study door flew open, for Beth had heard the commotion. Joy gave her strength, and she ran straight into her father's arms.

Mr March told his family how he had longed to surprise them, and how his doctor had let him come home early. He praised Brooke's devotion and care, glancing over at Meg as he spoke. But she was poking the fire, and did not look up.

The Christmas dinner was splendid, with a fat stuffed turkey, plum-pudding, and jellies. Mr Laurence, Laurie, and Mr Brooke dined with the Marches, and everyone gave toasts, told stories, and sang songs.

"Just a year ago we were groaning over a dismal Christmas," Jo reminded her sisters.

"I'm glad the year is over, because we've got Father back now," Beth declared.

Mr March smiled at his daughters. "Rather a rough road for you to travel, my little pilgrims," he said. "But you have got on bravely, and I think the burdens are likely to tumble off very soon."

An Alcott homecoming
Louisa May Alcott's father was often away on lecture tours, and, like Marmee and the March sisters, the Alcott women got used to looking after themselves. But Father's homecoming was always a celebration.

The tall man's loving family recognized him immediately!

Chapter eleven

Aunt march settles the question

*John Brooke's sudden
arrival put Meg's plan to
the test.*

Seeing Meg at the parlour window the next day, Laurie fell down on one knee, clasping his hands.

"That's how your John will go on, by and by," Jo said crossly.

"Don't plague me," pleaded Meg. "I can't say or do anything until John speaks."

"If he did, you'd cry or blush instead of saying no," Jo said.

"I'd say, 'Thank you, Mr Brooke, you are very kind. But I am too young to be married, so please say no more.'"

John Brooke's sudden arrival put Meg's plan to the test sooner than expected.

"I came to see how your father is," he said, as Jo slipped out of the room.

Meg stepped towards the door. "Mother will like to see you. I'll call her," she murmured.

"Don't go. Are you afraid of me, Margaret?" Mr Brooke asked.

Meg liked to hear him say her name. "How can I be afraid, when you have been so kind to Father?" she replied gratefully.

Mr Brooke looked down at Meg with so much love in his brown eyes that her heart fluttered. "I only want to know if you care for me a little, Meg. I love you so much."

Meg forgot every word of her planned speech, and instead murmured, "I don't know."

John took hold of her hands. "You could learn to like me. I love to teach, and this is easier than German." His eyes were merry, and he wore what seemed to Meg to be a smug smile.

This nettled her, and she pulled away. "Please go away and let me be!" she said.

Mr Brooke was bewildered. "Perhaps you'll change your mind?" he asked anxiously. "I'll wait till you've had more time."

At that moment, Aunt March hobbled in. "Who's this?" cried the old lady.

"It's Father's friend, Mr Brooke," stammered Meg, as John vanished into the study.

"I know all about it," Aunt March said sharply. "Tell me, do you mean to marry him? If so, not one penny of my money ever goes to you."

Her words roused Meg's spirit.

"I shall marry whom I please, Aunt March, and you can leave your money to anyone you like," Meg said. She suddenly felt brave and independent.

"My dear, be reasonable. You ought to marry well and help your family. It's your duty," Aunt March pointed out.

"My John is willing to work. He is energetic and brave. Everyone likes and respects him, and I'm proud he cares for me," said Meg earnestly. "I'm not afraid of being poor, for I've been happy so far. He loves me and – "

Then she remembered that she had told John to go away. Aunt March was angry. She had set her heart on her pretty niece making a fine match. "I wash my hands of the whole affair," she declared, slamming the door as she left the room. Meg was unsure whether to laugh or cry.

"I wash my hands of the whole affair," Aunt March declared.

Anna's announcement
When her sister, Anna, got engaged to John Pratt, Louisa May Alcott wrote in her journal, "I'd never forgive J for taking Anna away … but I shall if he makes her happy."

"I couldn't help hearing, Meg!" John exclaimed, coming into the parlour. "Thank you for defending me, and proving that you do care for me a little bit. May I stay and be happy, dear?"

Here was another chance to make her speech, but Meg simply whispered, "Yes, John."

Fifteen minutes later, Jo paused outside the parlour door. Hearing nothing, she smiled and went inside, assuming that Meg had sent John away as planned.

But Jo's mouth fell open when she beheld the enemy, with Meg on his knee. Meg jumped up, looking both proud and shy. John Brooke laughed and said, "Sister Jo, congratulate us!"

Jo rushed upstairs to report the awful news to her parents and sisters. Mr and Mrs March hastened downstairs. Both Amy and Beth thought the news of the engagement most agreeable.

A great deal of talking went on in the parlour that afternoon. Mr Brooke pleaded his case, told of his plans, and persuaded his friends to agree. He proudly took Meg in to supper. They looked so happy that Jo hadn't the heart to be dismal. Amy admired John's devotion and Meg's dignity, and Beth beamed at them. Their parents watched the young couple with tender satisfaction.

"Joys come close upon the sorrows this time," said Mrs March. "In most families there comes, now and then, a year full of events. This has been one, but it ends well after all."

"Hope the next will end better," muttered Jo.

When the group went into the parlour to greet Mr Laurence, Laurie followed Jo into a corner. "You don't look very festive, ma'am. What's the matter?" he asked.

"You can't know how hard it is for me to give up Meg," said Jo, with a little quiver in her voice. "I've lost my dearest friend."

"It will be all right," Laurie said consolingly. "Meg is happy; Brooke will get settled with Grandpa's help. We'll have capital times after she is gone, for I shall be through college before long. Don't you wish you could look forward and see where we shall all be in three years?"

Jo's eyes went slowly round the room, taking in the pleasant scene. Her parents sat together, observing the new romance that was blossoming. Amy was drawing Meg and John, while Beth lay on the sofa chatting with Mr Laurence.

"No, I don't want to know where we shall all be," Jo said at last. "I might see something sad. And everyone looks so happy now, I don't believe they could be much improved."

"Everyone looks so happy now, I don't believe they could be much improved."

THE REAL JO MARCH

Louisa May Alcott (1832–88) was a woman ahead of her time. Her main ambition was to relieve her family's financial worries. As a child, she had a talent for making up stories, and eventually succeeded in using her writing skills to support her family. At a time when women were beginning to campaign for political and social rights, Louisa brought their inner thoughts and ambitions into the public eye through characters like Jo March.

Orchard House today

Louisa May Alcott
"I *will* make a way in this rough and tumble world," Louisa vowed, and she did. At age 35, she achieved financial security and fame with the publication of *Little Women*.

Anna (Meg)
Louisa's older sister, Anna, was a quiet, agreeable girl. She married John Pratt in 1860 and they had two sons, Frederick and John.

Elizabeth (Beth)
Elizabeth was ill for two years before she died in 1858. Louisa was devastated, but grateful that her sister was no longer in pain.

May (Amy)
May became a painter in Paris, but died soon after having a baby in 1879. Louisa raised May's daughter, Lulu, in Massachusetts.

Abba (Marmee)
Louisa's mother, Abba, understood her strong-willed nature. They were both practical women who worked hard to support the family.

Father
Bronson Alcott had a vision for an ideal world, but often ignored the realities of life. When Louisa was 11, the family lived on a commune according to his rules for a perfect world. The commune lasted for one year.

Orchard House
The Alcotts lived at Orchard House in Concord, Massachusetts for 20 years. Louisa used it as the model for the March family home. Orchard House is now a museum.

Concord, Massachusetts
Concord attracted many intellectuals, such as the writers Ralph Waldo Emerson, Henry David Thoreau and Nathaniel Hawthorne. They helped to kindle Louisa's curiosity and ambition.

Louisa loved the New England countryside around Concord.

Louisa's room was a private haven filled with her favourite things.

Louisa's desk
Louisa wrote at this desk in her bedroom at Orchard House. She liked to write quickly in a state of deep concentration that she called a "vortex".

Little Women
Louisa's sister, May, illustrated this first edition of *Little Women* in 1868. It took several more years of study – financed by Louisa – before May achieved success.

In Good Wives, Jo marries Professor Bhaer.

Good Wives
Published in 1869, *Little Women, Part 2* was later renamed *Good Wives*. In it, Jo gets married and is a successful writer.

Little Men
In *Little Men*, published in 1871, Jo and Professor Bhaer open a school based on Bronson Alcott's philosophy of "nourishing the mind".

Illustration from the first edition of Little Men.

Louisa May Alcott wrote many stories for both children and adults. Although she was a very practical person, in her stories Louisa enjoyed the fantasy world of fairy tales and romantic adventures. However, her best-known works – Little Women and its sequels – are based on her own life. After Little Women was published, fans asked if Jo and Laurie would get married. Though she wanted Jo to be independent like herself, Louisa compromised.

LITTLE WOMEN LIVE ON. . .

Though women today have much more freedom, Jo's struggle to be accepted while remaining true to herself is a timeless theme that applies to both women and men of any age. Jo's story has also become a favourite film. Several hit movie versions of Little Women have been made.

Jo is horrified by the state of Marmee's old slippers.

Oscar winner
The 1933 film of *Little Women* starred Katharine Hepburn as Jo. The film won an Academy Award for best script, and was also nominated for best picture.

Star-studded cast
The 1949 film starred June Allyson as Jo, Janet Leigh as Meg, Elizabeth Taylor as Amy, and Margaret O'Brien as Beth. All were top Hollywood stars of the day.

Acknowledgements

Picture credits

t = top, b = bottom, l = left, r = right, a = above, c = centre

Louisa May Alcott Memorial Association , Orchard House, Concord, Mass. 01742-0343, USA: 19tr, 28bl, 30bl,52bl, 62tl, cla, clb, bl, bla, 62tr, br, 63tl, cl, cr,

Bridgeman Art Library: 12t, cl, bl,13tl, cl, br, 16tl, 21tr, 23br, 26br, 33tr, 36tl, 42tl, 42-3b, 48bl, 53br, 59br,

Concord Free Public Library, Mass. USA: 39tl, 62bc,

Dorling Kindersley Picture Library: 20tl, 47tr, 54bl,

/Andy Crawford/Blists Hill Museum: 12br, 32bl,

/Dave King: 34bl, 56bl,

/Liz McAulay: 26tl,

/Clive Streeter: 41tr;

/Worthing Museum: 14bl,

Mary Evans Picture Library: 9tr, 10cl, 22bl, 28tl,36bl, 42c, 43tl, 46br,49tr, 63tr,

Ronald Grant Archive: 3, 63bl, br,

Hulton Getty Images: 42tr,

Kobal Collection: 6-7, 43br;

Museum of the Confederacy, Richmond, Virginia, USA: 435c;

Peter Newark Americana Pictures: 13 tr, cr,18tl, 42trb, 50,

Science & Society Picture Library: 45br, 47trb, cr;

Tony Stone Images: 52br;

US Army Military Historical Institute, Carlisle, Penn. USA: 43bc,

The Journals of Louisa May Alcott, ed. Joel Myerson and Daniel Shealy; associate editor, Madeleine B. Stern. Boston, Massachusetts: Little, Brown, 1989; reprinted, Athens, Georgia: University of Georgia Press, 1997.

Additional illustrations: Sallie Alane Reason

Dorling Kindersley would particularly like to thank the staff at Orchard House for assistance with research; Colleen Lynch and Natascha Biebow for editorial help.